D0579931

For our home—planet Earth,
spinning blue in the dark, surrounded by stars—
and for my family

BEACH LANE BOOKS
An imprint of Simon & Schuster Children's Publishing Division
1230 Avenue of the Americas, New York, New York 10020

The text for this book was set in Perpetua.
The illustrations for this book were rendered in watercolor, gouache, and colored pencil
on 150 lb. Arches cold press watercolor paper.
Manufactured in China
0522 SCP
First Edition
10 9 8 7 6 5 4 3 2 1
Library of Congress Cataloging-in-Publication Data
Names: Stringer, Lauren, author, illustrator.
Title: The Dark was done / Lauren Stringer.
Description: First edition. | New York : Beach Lane Books, [2022] | Audience: Ages 0–8. |
Audience: Grades 2–3. | Summary: A young boy puts aside his fear of the Dark and sets out to
bring it back, along with its music, magic, and mysteries.
Identifiers: LCCN 2021047688 (print) | LCCN 2021047689 (ebook) | ISBN 9781534462922
(hardcover) | ISBN 9781534462939 (ebook)
Subjects: CYAC: Light and darkness—Fiction. | Night—Fiction. | LCGFT: Picture books.
Classification: LCC PZ7.S9183 Dar 2022 (print) | LCC PZ7.S9183 (ebook) | DDC [E]—dc23
LC record available at https://lccn.loc.gov/2021047688
LC ebook record available at https://lccn.loc.gov/2021047689

DARK WAS DONE

Lauren Stringer

BEACH LANE BOOKS • New York London Toronto Sydney New Delhi

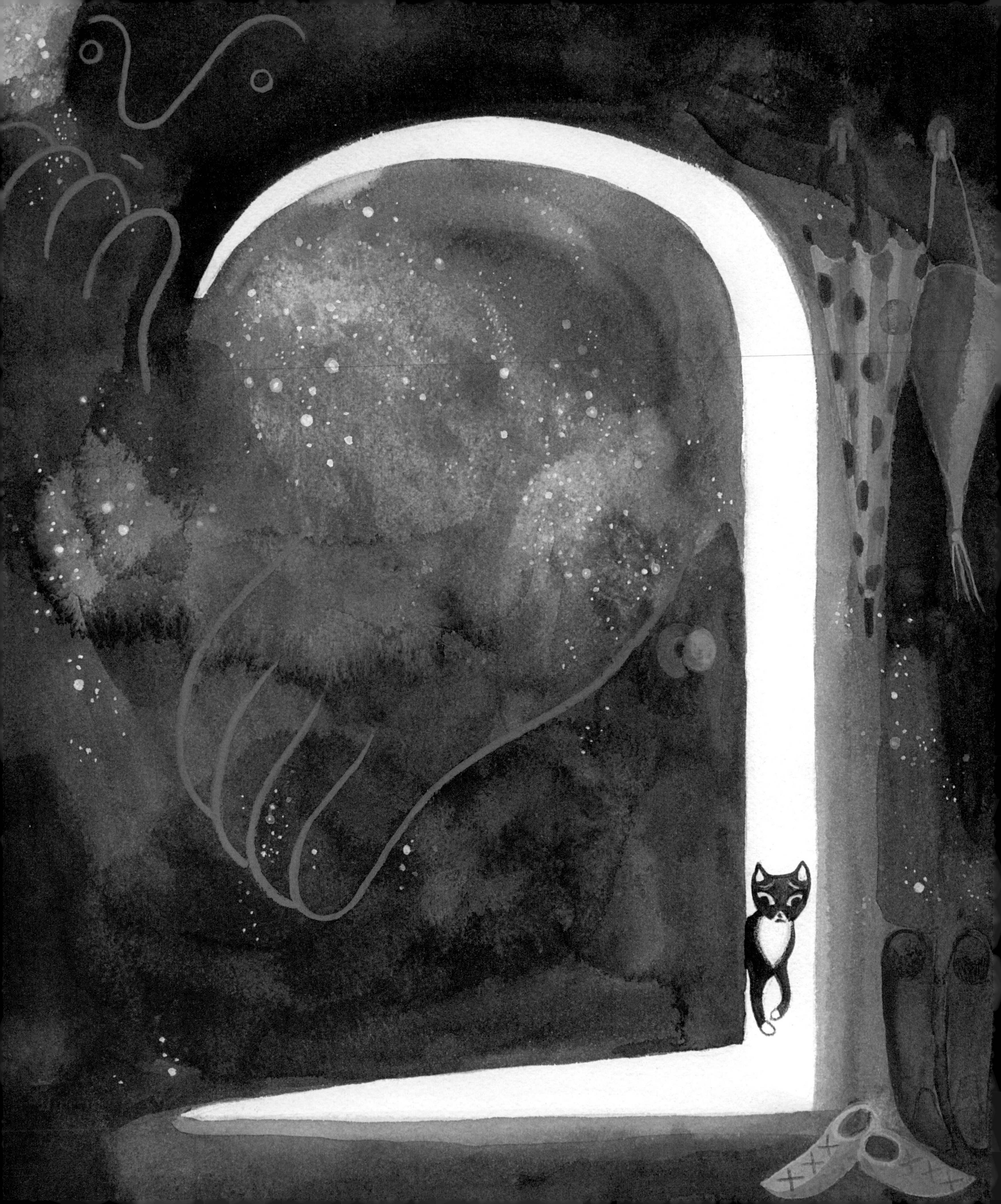

THE DARK was tired of hiding.

Nightlights, streetlights, flashlights, and table lamps—

all pushed the Dark away.

Everyone was afraid of the Dark.
Everyone wished the Dark would leave.

Even the boy who loved the song of crickets
was afraid of the Dark under his bed.
Even he wished the Dark would leave.

And so . . .
the Dark decided to go.
All the world over,
continent by continent,
ocean by ocean,
the Dark left and did not return.
The Dark was done.

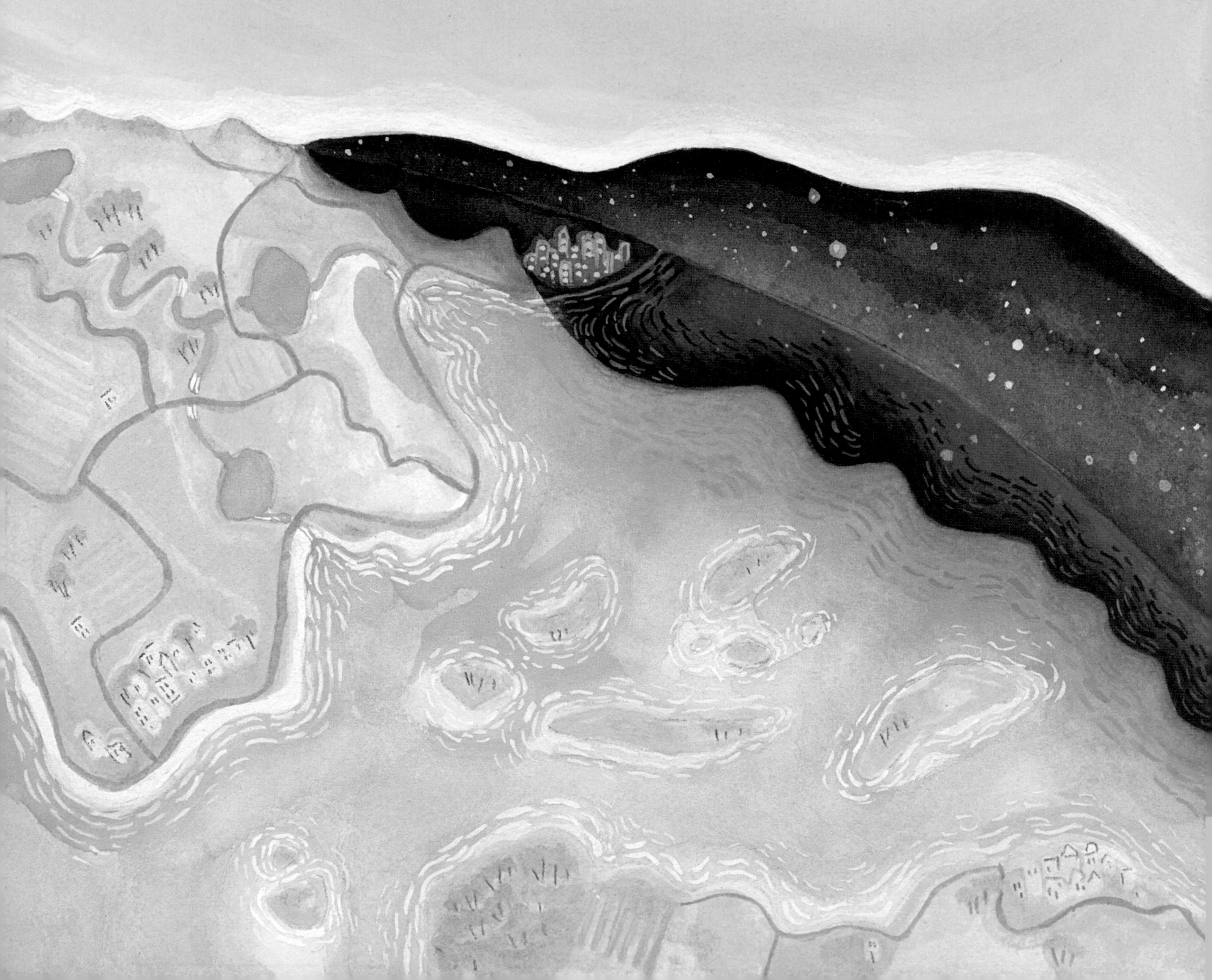

At first, nobody missed the Dark.
Everyone felt safe in the light.

Then one day—or maybe it was night,
no one could tell the difference—
the boy said, "I miss the song of crickets."

"Their song is a gift of the Dark," said his mother.
"When the Dark left, the crickets' song left too."

Then the boy said,
"I miss the hooting owls."

"The owls are night creatures and gifts of the Dark," said his father. "When the Dark left, the owls left too."

"And the flying bats?" asked the boy.

"And the flying bats too," said his father.

Then the boy said, "I miss the twinkling stars."

"The twinkling stars are a gift of the Dark
and come out only at night," said his mother.

"When the Dark left, the stars left too," said his father.

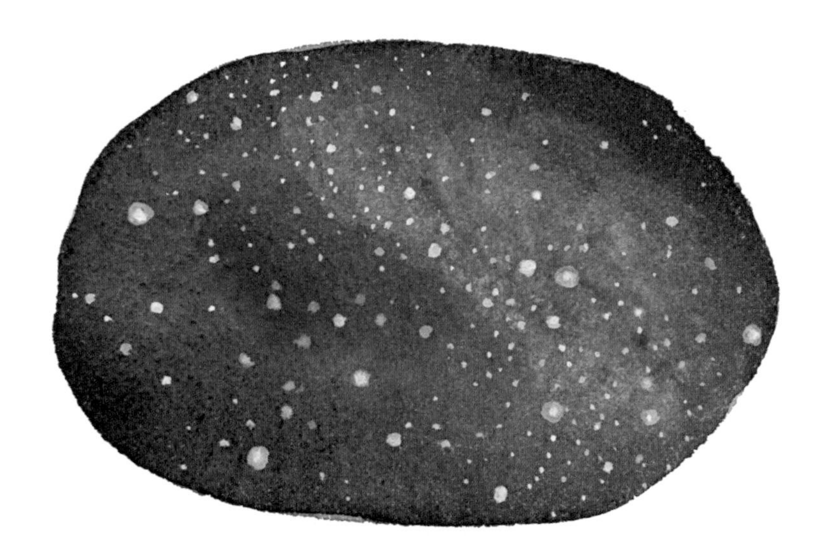

"I want to go look for the Dark," said the boy.

"But you are afraid of the Dark," said his parents.

The boy thought for a moment, then said,
"If the Dark gives us the song of crickets
and hooting owls, flying bats
and twinkling stars . . .

then I am no longer afraid of the Dark.
I am going to find the Dark and persuade the Dark to return."

The boy looked for the Dark
in all the Dark's places
but found only light.
And then he met a burglar.

"Where are you going?" asked the burglar.

"I miss the song of crickets and hooting owls,
flying bats and twinkling stars," said the boy.
"I am going to find the Dark and persuade the Dark to return."

"I miss shadows to hide in," said the burglar. "May I come with you?"

The boy did not mind.
In the light, the burglar did not look scary.

So the boy and the burglar set off together to look for the Dark and came upon a poet sitting in the middle of the road.

“Where are you going?” asked the poet.

“We miss the song of crickets and hooting owls,
flying bats and twinkling stars,” said the boy.

“And shadows to hide in,” said the burglar.
“We are going to find the Dark and persuade the Dark to return.”

“There is no mystery without the Dark,” said the poet.
“Without mystery I cannot write a poem. May I come with you?”

So the boy, the burglar, and the poet set off together
to look for the Dark.

Then by the side of the road they met a gardener.
When she heard where they were going, she said,
"I miss the scent of night-blooming jasmine.
It only flowers in the Dark.
May I come with you?"

So the boy, the burglar, the poet, and the gardener
continued down the road to find the Dark,
to persuade the Dark to return.

And when others learned where they were going, they joined them.
Soon a long parade of people who missed the song of crickets,
hooting owls, flying bats, twinkling stars,
shadows to hide in, mysteries for poems,
and the scent of night-blooming jasmine
filled the road from near to far.

“Keep your ears open for the song of crickets!” cried the boy.

“Keep your eyes open for shadows to hide in!” cried the burglar.

“Keep your heart open to the mysteries!” cried the poet.

“Keep your nose open for the scent of night-blooming jasmine!” cried the gardener.

Hearing everyone's cries,
the Dark felt persuaded to return.
As the night fell
and the light disappeared,
everyone cowered in fear.
Even the burglar was afraid.

But then an owl hooted and a bat flew by.
The boy heard the song of crickets and opened
his eyes to the twinkling stars.
The boy and the Dark hugged each other,
and the scent of night-blooming jasmine filled the air.

Everyone breathed in the scent and smiled.
The boy, the burglar, the poet, the gardener,
and the long parade of people—
all welcomed back the Dark.

And so . . .
each night,
all the world over,
continent by continent,
ocean by ocean,
the Dark eagerly returned.

And each night when the boy heard the song of crickets,
he waved good night to the Dark under his bed,
then turned out the light . . .

and the Dark felt welcomed—
and loved.